Having captured the hearts and imaginations
of millions of fans around the world, it's no surprise
that *Frozen* is one of the most popular animated movies
of all time. Now, join Anna and Elsa for a brand-new
adventure, as the magic continues in *Frozen 2*!

AUTUMN
PUBLISHING

Published in 2019
by Autumn Publishing
Cottage Farm
Sywell
NN6 0BJ
www.igloobooks.com

Autumn is an imprint of Bonnier Books UK

0919 001
2 4 6 8 10 9 7 5 3 1
ISBN 978-1-78905-163-6

Printed and manufactured in China

PLATINUM COLLECTION

Disney
FROZEN II

 AUTUMN
PUBLISHING

Elsa, the queen of Arendelle, tries to do the best for her people. She has always wondered why she has powers and where they came from. When a voice starts calling to her, Elsa wonders if she'll finally learn the truth.

Anna is a strong, confident young woman. She cares
deeply for her sister, Elsa, and would do anything for
her. With the safety of Arendelle at stake, Anna joins her
sister on a journey north to put things right.

Considered a member of the family, Kristoff is
always on hand to help Elsa and the love of his life, Anna.
During their adventures in the Enchanted Forest, Kristoff
starts to wonder if Anna's future will include him.

Sven is living proof that reindeer are better than people. He is Kristoff's best friend and the only one the ice-harvester trusts with a big secret regarding his relationship with Anna.

Just over three years have passed since Elsa brought
Olaf to life. The friendly snowman who likes warm hugs
is fascinated with every aspect of life. Having recently
learnt to read, Olaf is always full of questions.

Lieutenant Destin Mattias has been trapped in the
Enchanted Forest for over 30 years. Totally loyal to
Arendelle, Mattias finds the magical powers of his new
queen the first of many challenges to his beliefs.

Gale is the Wind Spirit who Elsa, Anna
and the rest of the group encounter when they
first enter the Enchanted Forest. It can seem
playful, but it is a powerful spirit.

Bruni is the Fire Spirit who Elsa meets in the
Enchanted Forest. It appears at times of unrest and
leaves a trail of fire wherever it goes. Only Elsa is able
to calm the small creature and put out its flames.

The Earth Giants are the Earth Spirits inside the
Enchanted Forest. Often mistaken for mountains and
hills when sleeping, they become extremely grumpy
when awake. It's best to leave them alone.

The Water Spirit, also known as the Water Nokk, is guardian of secrets within the forest. A person must show they are worthy in order to learn the secrets that the Water Nokk protects. Will Elsa be able to prove herself?

Many years ago, young princesses Anna and Elsa loved listening to their parents' stories about the past. One night, King Agnarr told them about the Northuldra, people from an enchanted forest.

The Northuldra had lived in harmony with the people of Arendelle, but then everything changed and the two sides went to war. Angered spirits trapped both sides in the forest, but King Agnarr managed to escape.

"Were the Northuldra magical, like me?" asked Elsa, curiously.

But her parents didn't have the answer.

Queen Iduna soothed her daughters to sleep with a lullaby about a special river called Ahtohallan. Legend said the river held all the answers about the past.

"Do you think Ahtohallan knows why I have powers?" asked Elsa.

"If Ahtohallan is out there, I imagine it knows that and much more," answered the queen.

"Someone should really try to find it," said Elsa, as she closed her eyes and drifted off to sleep.

Later, Anna woke up and ran to the window. She looked out excitedly at the Northern Lights, before calling to Elsa.

"The sky's awake. So I'm awake. So we have to play."

And so they did.

Many playtimes and many years went by since that moment under the Northern Lights. Though their parents were gone, Anna and Elsa always cared for each other, even when circumstances forced them apart as they grew up.

Now, with Elsa the queen of Arendelle, the sisters were closer than ever. They also had a group of friends – Kristoff, Olaf and Sven – who were like family to them.

Though their lives were busy, the one thing the friends always made time for was family games night. Tonight, they were playing charades.

It was Elsa's turn, but Anna struggled to guess what her sister was acting out and knew something was bothering her. "Are you okay?" asked Anna.

"Just tired," replied Elsa, forcing a smile. "Goodnight," she added, as she abruptly left and went upstairs.

Moments later Anna arrived to check on Elsa.

"You're wearing Mother's scarf," she said to Elsa, concerned. "You do that when something's wrong."

Elsa didn't want to worry Anna, but something was wrong. A voice was calling to her. It seemed as though no one else could hear it, but it tugged at her, as if trying to draw her out of the kingdom.

Though she tried with all her might, she couldn't silence it.

Later that night, Elsa
was woken up by the
mysterious voice. It was
calling to her once again.
As much as she wanted it
to stop, she also couldn't
help feeling curious –
did the voice belong to
someone magical, like her?

She sang in response to
the voice and a thought
came to her. She carefully
used her magic to toss
snow out into the air.
Images she had never
seen before blossomed
from her fingertips and
surrounded her.

Fascinated, Elsa blasted out her magic and an enormous shock wave shot across the fjord!

The rain froze into small crystals that hung suspended in the air!

Elsa looked around, stunned and frightened by what she had done.

The deafening sound startled Anna awake and she raced to the balcony, searching for Elsa.

As their eyes met, a blast of blinding light came from the north and the crystals dropped to the ground.

As the crystals fell, Arendelle transformed.
Water stopped flowing, fire vanished, the
wind kicked up and pushed villagers out
of their homes, then the ground rippled
like the sea!

Through the chaos, Anna and Kristoff led
everyone up to the cliffs.

Once everyone was safely above Arendelle,
Elsa told Anna about the voice.

She explained that the voice had shown
her the Enchanted Forest. Elsa knew she
needed to travel there.

"I'm going with you," insisted Anna.

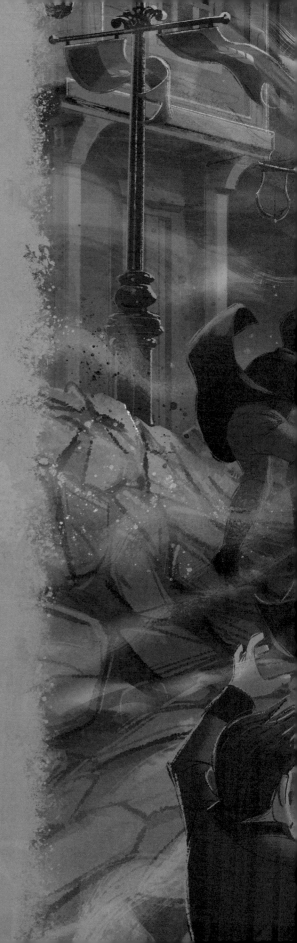

The ground rumbled again, but this time it was the mountain trolls rolling through the pass. Grand Pabbie went straight to Elsa. Both of them could feel that the spirits of nature were angry.

He explained there was a great wrong that needed mending. Without it being fixed, Pabbie could see no future. "When one can see no future, all one can do is the next right thing," he added.

To do that, Elsa knew she needed to find the voice. "And for the first time, Anna, I am not afraid," she said.

Grand Pabbie motioned to Anna and told her that he would take care of the villagers, but she needed to watch over Elsa. "I won't let anything happen to her," Anna promised.

At dawn, Anna, Kristoff, Olaf and Sven joined Elsa, and they began their long journey north. They passed many places they had seen before and continued even further into the unknown.

As the day turned to evening, everyone was tired of Olaf's ceaseless chatter. Since he had learnt to read, he had been full of fun facts, and he felt that their trip was the perfect excuse to share them all.

"Did you know that water has memory?" Olaf asked. "Did you know men are six times more likely to be struck by lightning? Sorry, Kristoff!"

As the night came to an end, Elsa asked Kristoff to stop the sleigh. "I hear it. I hear the voice," she said.

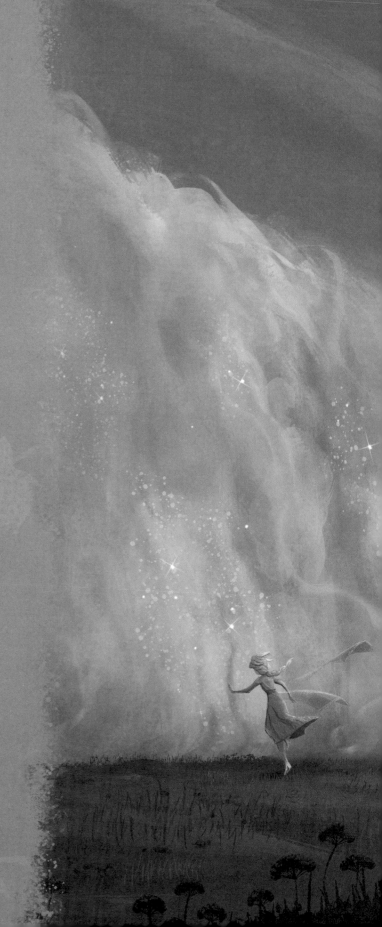

Up ahead, over a small rise in the road, was a vast wall of glittering mist. Elsa stopped a safe distance away, saying nothing as her friends joined her.

Kristoff and Olaf were far less patient. As they neared the mist, Kristoff raised his hand and touched it. The group watched as his hand sprang back towards him.

Olaf made a run for it, and bounced off like he was hitting a balloon. He giggled and did it over and over again.

Elsa reached for Anna's hand, drawing on her sister's strength. Slowly the mist parted before them.

"Promise me we'll do this together," Anna said.

Elsa replied, "I promise."

The mist continued to roll back, revealing four stone monoliths,
each with a symbol carved into it. As they passed the pillars, the mist
closed behind Elsa, Anna and their friends, trapping them inside!

The sparkling colours in the mist shifted and aligned, and something
about it changed. When they reached out and touched it, the mist
pushed back.

Suddenly, they were propelled
free of the mist and into a
clearing. "What was that?"
Kristoff asked.

Olaf touched the mist they
had just emerged from. It had
returned to being bouncy.

"Well, it let us in, but it clearly
doesn't want to let us out,"
Kristoff said.

"Bright side, the forest is
beautiful," Elsa added.

With the soft rays of the sun
illuminating the forest, it was
like walking through a dream.
The towering trees, with their
shimmering golden leaves,
stretched towards the sky.

The group slowed their pace,
staggered by the beauty all
around them.

After exploring the forest for
a little while, the Wind Spirit
appeared, picking up Olaf as if
he was as light as a feather! The
strength of the current broke him
into pieces, whirling him round
and round.

As everyone tried to help they got
swept up in the wind storm, too!

Elsa used her magic to stop a
branch from slamming into
Anna, which caused the Wind
Spirit to push everyone but Elsa
out of its grasp. Desperately,
Elsa threw a steady stream of
snow towards the centre of the
swirling vortex.

The wind swirled tightly around Elsa until finally, she opened her arms, blasting out her powers. Snow filled the air and froze into beautiful ice sculptures.

Each one appeared to represent a moment in time. Elsa had never created anything like it before.

"Water has memory," said Olaf, explaining to everyone why the ice sculptures were showing moments from the past.

With Elsa finally free, the group studied the sculptures. One of them in particular captured their attention – it was Elsa and Anna's father when he was younger, cradled in the arms of a Northuldra girl!

Suddenly, they heard noises
coming from the bushes. Anna
broke off an ice sword from one
of Elsa's sculptures. Before they
knew it, they were surrounded
by a group of people, including
soldiers. It was the trapped
Northuldra and Arendellians
from King Agnarr's story!

Still at odds after so many years,
the leader of the Northuldra,
Yelana, immediately began
bickering with the Arendellian
lieutenant, Mattias.

Anna took a step forwards. Suddenly, believing she was about to attack, both the Northuldra and the Arendellians rushed towards the group. Elsa used her powers to send them all slipping to the ground.

"That was magic," said Mattias. "Did you see that?"

"Of course I saw it," Yelana responded.

Olaf went over to greet one of the Northuldra. His name was Ryder. He introduced his sister, Honeymaren, to the talking snowman and the rest of the group.

Anna stared at Mattias, trying to figure out where she knew him from.

Finally, she blurted, "Library, second portrait on the left. You were our father's official guard."

He was overjoyed to hear their father was King Agnarr and that he had made it back to Arendelle.

Yelana burst forwards, wanting to know what sorcery the girls had used to come through the mist and awaken the spirits. Anna explained that Elsa had been born with magic.

"Did you know that your grandfather, your king, despised magic?" Yelana asked.

"He only feared how people like you could exploit it!" Mattias responded. "The spirits turned against you for your actions!"

"You are trapped here, too!" Yelana shouted back.

Out of nowhere, a bright flash appeared.

"Fire Spirit!" Yelana yelled.

The ball of fire dashed around a tree, sending it up in flames. Chaos erupted as it blazed a trail through the forest, burning everything in its path.

Elsa raced behind it, using her magic to try and stop the fire from spreading.

When she finally managed to chase it down, she saw that the Fire Spirit was a small salamander.

Looking deep into its terrified eyes, she understood its feelings of pain and fear. She gently held out her hand and it scampered onto it, enjoying her cool touch. As she calmed the Fire Spirit down, the flames died.

Moments later, Elsa heard the voice that had been calling out to her. The salamander heard it, too, and helped Elsa realise she had to travel even further north.

When Anna reached Elsa, they held each other tightly. Anna was angry that Elsa had put herself in danger by chasing the flames. But both of them were grateful to be safe – if only for the moment.

Elsa pulled out their mother's scarf and wrapped it around Anna, knowing it would comfort her. Ryder and Honeymaren were intrigued by it. Elsa explained that it had been a gift from their father to their mother. It had been one of her most cherished possessions.

Recognising the symbols on the scarf, Ryder took the sisters back to the ice sculptures Elsa had created. Elsa compared their mother's scarf to the one the young girl was wearing. They were identical. The girl who had saved their father had been Northuldra.

The two opposing sides were bewildered by the discovery of the sacrifice one enemy had made for another. Suddenly, their differences, anger and suspicions melted away.

When everyone had gathered together for stew and glogg, Anna began talking to Mattias. He shared with Anna some wisdom he had learnt from his father. "Just when you think you've found your way, life'll throw you onto a new path."

Anna knew what came after that – a person just needed to do the next right thing.

Meanwhile, Honeymaren was explaining the symbols on Elsa's scarf. "Air, fire, water and earth," she said, pointing at each of them. She pointed out a fifth spirit, said to be a bridge between people and the magic of nature. "Some say they heard it call out the day the forest fell," she added.

"My father heard it. Do you think that's who's calling me?" asked Elsa.

"Maybe. Alas, only Ahtohallan knows," replied Honeymaren.

Elsa was now certain that she had to follow the call to set everyone free.

Later on, Elsa took Anna to one side and told her sister she had decided to follow the voice even further north. Anna refused to let her go alone.

Anna desperately looked around for Kristoff, but couldn't find him anywhere. Holding back tears, Anna asked Yelana to pass a message to Kristoff. She then headed north with Elsa and Olaf.

Yelana found Kristoff in a clearing. She passed on the message from Anna that she'd headed north with Elsa.

Left alone in the clearing, Kristoff struggled to believe Anna had left without him. He walked sadly through the forest, trying to sort out his feelings and wondering whether or not he had a place in Anna's future.

Further north, Elsa led Anna and Olaf up a large hill, as she followed the mysterious voice.

Soon they were looking down at an old Arendellian shipwreck, its tattered flag waving sadly in the wind.

Anna and Elsa ran down to take a closer look. They gasped when they realised it was their parents' ship!

All three of them ran
down to take a closer look,
making sure to search the
wreck carefully from top
to bottom. They soon
discovered a map that proved
their parents had been trying
to find Ahtohallan.

Using her magic, Elsa pulled
moisture from the old ship
and created ice sculptures
like those she created back in
the forest.

As the Wind Spirit swept
past each sculpture, they
revealed the story of their
parents' journey.

Voices from the past echoed,
showing Elsa, Anna and Olaf
that the king and queen were
seeking answers about Elsa's
magic when the crashing
waves overcame them.

Overwhelmed with guilt,
Elsa decided she had to
continue alone. She waved
her hands, creating an ice
boat, and sent Anna and
Olaf sliding down a hill.

Anna tried to stop the boat
and thought she had been
successful as it changed
course and slid across
dry land.

But when it dropped down
a slope, Anna and Olaf
slipped into a river of
sleeping Earth Giants.

"Hang on, Olaf," said Anna.
Using a branch, she directed
their boat away from the
Earth Giants, only to drop
down a waterfall!

Meanwhile, Elsa had finally reached the Dark Sea. She narrowed her eyes as she looked with determination past the mountainous waves to the other side.

Taking a deep breath, she sprinted onto the sea, creating snowflakes at her feet. But the strength of the waves quickly knocked her down.

Elsa pulled herself back to the shore and leapt onto a nearby boulder. As a wave came towards her, she froze it and used it as a slide, but the next wave smashed it to pieces and she dived into the water.

She had no time to notice the enormous Water Nokk watching her...

Deep beneath the dark waters,
a lightning flash illuminated
the Water Nokk. It swam up to
Elsa and looked her in the eye
before disappearing in the next
lightning strike.

Elsa pulled herself to the top
of the water and climbed onto
some floating ice she created.
The Water Nokk surfaced at
speed and rammed the ice,
breaking it and tossing Elsa
back into the water.

The two battled, both above
and under the raging sea, but
then Elsa used her magic to
make an ice bridle. She grabbed
the reins and swung onto the
Water Nokk's back. At first it
bucked, but soon she was riding
it to the opposite shore.

Once safely across the Dark Sea, Elsa removed the bridle from the Water Nokk. Her journey was at an end!

The mysterious voice was now silent, and for the first time in her life, Elsa felt completely at ease.

Her adventures in the north had changed her, freed her. Elsa had no doubt that peace and harmony were finally going to be restored to the unbalanced land.

Across the sea, Anna and Olaf's boat landed them in lost caverns.
They got out and explored their surroundings, illuminated by Anna's
torch. Suddenly, an ice sculpture began to form before their eyes!
They were relieved. This meant Elsa had made it across the Dark Sea!

Anna looked closely at the ice sculpture, and she immediately knew why Elsa had sent it as a message. It explained what had happened in the forest all those years ago. Anna wondered how she could correct all the wrongs of the past. Then she remembered the advice given to her by Mattias – do the next right thing.

So with that, Anna took a step forwards, confident that Arendelle would soon be safe again, and the people trapped in the Enchanted Forest would be set free…